14 45

PASSOVER MAGIC

Written by Roni Schotter   Illustrated by Marylin Hafner

Little, Brown and Company
Boston New York Toronto London

For Geoffrey and Lizzie, Andy and Anne, Harvey and Sara,
and for Vicki Ettenger, with thanks
— R. S.

For my beloved brother Everett
— M. H.

Also by Roni Schotter and Marylin Hafner:
Hanukkah!

First Edition

Library of Congress Cataloging-in-Publication Data

Schotter, Roni.
   Passover magic / written by Roni Schotter ; illustrated by Marylin
Hafner. — 1st ed.
      p.   cm.
   Summary: A young girl and her relatives celebrate Passover with
the traditional seder, a dinner with special foods and special
meaning.
   ISBN 0-316-77468-5
   [1. Passover — Fiction.   2. Jews — Fiction.]   I. Hafner, Marylin,
ill.   II. Title.
PZ7.S3765Pas   1995
[E] — dc20   93-20053

10 9 8 7 6 5 4 3 2 1

NIL

Published simultaneously in Canada by Little, Brown & Company (Canada) Limited
and in Great Britain by Little, Brown and Company (UK) Limited

Printed in Italy

Something magical happens every spring. The last white of winter fades from the ground, grass greens, and out of nowhere, flowers appear. Passover comes and with it, the relatives!

For a week Ben and I have helped clean the house, and now we are ready. Everyone is coming a day early. Grandma and Grandpa arrive first with smiles and hugs. Together, we are crumb detectives. Soon the house is Passover perfect.

Later Uncle Bernie arrives with kisses and complaints, Aunt Ina with wine and worries, Cousin Sara with shouts, Max with his bear, Uncle Arnold with yawns. Our house is crowded and close. We are rich in relatives.

In the morning everyone rushes to get ready. Ben hunts for his belt.
Max won't wear his tie. "Too tight!" he cries. Sara can't find her barrette,
and I have lost my ribbon. Grandma and Mama start the chicken and the
chicken soup, and soon the house is sweet with the smell of Passover.

"Where's Harry?" Aunt Ina worries. Uncle Harry is coming from far away with our new Aunt Eda. Everyone loves Uncle Harry. During the week Uncle Harry is a dentist, pulling teeth out of people's mouths. On the weekends he's a magician, pulling rabbits out of people's hats. Mama says Eda used to be Uncle Harry's assistant. She says they fell in love the very first time Uncle Harry sawed Eda in half.

"Anybody home?" someone yells.

"Uncle Harry!" we all shout and rush to the door.

There he is, short and round and wearing a bright red bow tie. And there, beside him, is our new Aunt Eda, big and sparkling and very beautiful.

"This is my lucky charm — this is my Eda," Uncle Harry proudly proclaims.

"Sara! Benjamin!" he calls out suddenly. "What's this I see?"

Everyone gasps when Uncle Harry waves his large hand through the air and pulls Sara's barrette out of her ear and Ben's belt from inside his sleeve.

"Now, Max, they tell me you hate wearing ties, but maybe because it's Passover you'll wear one anyway." He opens his hands. Inside them are two red bow ties exactly like the one he is wearing. "One for you and one for your bear."

Everyone laughs and applauds. I look down at my shoes. I have
polished them so well that I can see my sad face reflected in them.
I am the oldest so, of course, Uncle Harry has nothing for me.

"Molly," I hear him say, "give me your hand."

I do, and Uncle Harry turns it over. There is the most beautiful hair
ribbon I've ever seen. "Uncle Harry!" I exclaim. "Thank you!"

But Uncle Harry has already turned to Grandma. He gives her a hug and pulls a bouquet of flowers from behind her back.

"For you, Mama. For the table. For Passover," he says.

"Oh, Harry!" Grandma laughs, her eyes full of love. "How do you do it?"

"It's Eda," Uncle Harry says. "She's my inspiration."

For the next few hours, we talk — everyone tells everyone everything — and in between, we work.

Grandma checks the chicken soup. Uncle Bernie sets the table with the special Passover china.

Papa and Grandpa roast a bone and an egg for the seder plate and arrange the parsley, horseradish, and salt water. Even Uncle Arnold helps.

Aunt Eda, her long nails gleaming, chops apples and nuts while Mama mixes in the cinnamon and wine to make delicious *haroses*. Ben, Sara, Max, and I mold matzoh balls from Aunt Ina's special mixture.

And Uncle Harry? He waves his magic hands over everything, saying, "The magic food of Passover. Once it's on the table, it disappears."

The sleepy spring sun has finally set. At last we are ready. It's time for the seder, our special holiday meal, to begin.

We open the Haggadahs, which tell the Passover story, and together whisper a blessing. Grandpa washes his hands in a special bowl. We dip the parsley into salt water and say thank you for all the green growing things of the earth.

Then comes the part I've been waiting for.... Grandpa reaches into the stack of three matzohs, the special flat bread of Passover. He pulls out the middle piece, the *afikomen* — but instead of putting half into his lap the way he always does, he winks and gives it instead to...Uncle Harry!

Uncle Harry is going to hide the *afikomen* this year. Whoever finds it gets a prize. Usually it's easy to find. But if Uncle Harry hides it... well, who can tell?

Uncle Harry smiles mysteriously and puts the special matzoh in his lap. It's time for Max to ask the Four Questions. "Why is this night different from all other nights? Why do we eat matzoh instead of bread?" he begins. With one eye I watch as Sara helps Max read. With the other I keep an eye on Uncle Harry.

Uncle Harry never moves from his chair. He does exactly what everyone else does — he reads aloud the words in Hebrew and English that answer Max's questions and tell how the Jews were freed from slavery in Egypt, and, when Grandpa says it's time, he sips the sweet wine the grown-ups drink while Ben, Sara, Max, and I sip our grape juice.

We read, we sip, we pray, and we taste the foods from the seder plate —
dipping the sharp horseradish into the sweet *haroses* to remember the
bitterness of slavery and the sweetness of freedom.

Then, finally, it's time to eat — fish and chicken and matzoh ball soup
and sweet potatoes and mountains and mountains of *haroses*. And just as
Uncle Harry said it would, the food disappears. But still Uncle Harry never
rises from his chair.

"Too much!" Uncle Bernie complains, holding his stomach.

"Maybe the matzoh balls were too heavy?" Aunt Ina worries.

"They were perfect, Ina," Uncle Bernie answers. "Like pillows. Feather pillows." Uncle Arnold yawns.

I am sleepy, too, my eyelids heavy, but I must keep them open. I have to watch Uncle Harry.

"Time to hunt!" Papa calls out, startling me.

Ben, Sara, Max, and I run to Uncle Harry to search his lap for the *afikomen,* the special matzoh. Nothing. Ben searches his pockets. Nothing. How did he do it?

In cupboards, under chairs, we search everywhere; we find nothing.

"Harry," Grandpa pleads, "tell them, are they warm?"

"My assistant will tell them," Uncle Harry says, smiling at Aunt Eda.

"Sara, Max, and Ben are winter cold," Aunt Eda says. "Molly is summer sizzling."

I am near the curtains. Excited, I push them aside. Nothing!

Uncle Harry looks surprised. "It should be there," he says, finally getting up from his chair. He searches behind the curtains and scratches his head. "Hmmm. Something's wrong," he says. "We need magic — a spell. Ben, Sara, Max, and Molly, help me. Close your eyes. Concentrate. Picture Passover. Say what you see."

I close my eyes so tight they hurt. I concentrate on Passover. I see the seder table full of food and my relatives full of love. Then I see my ancestors, hurrying across the desert, escaping from slavery, full of...

"Hope," I say out loud.

"Freedom," I hear Ben whisper.

HOPE

FREEDOM

"Family," Sara says softly.
(For once, she doesn't shout.)

"Food." Max giggles.

PESACH

"Perfect!" Uncle Harry says, and we open our eyes.

We yank the curtain aside and there, where it wasn't before, is the matzoh! Sara snatches it and shouts, "Presents!"

The grown-ups laugh, and Aunt Eda hands Uncle Harry a handkerchief. He waves it through the air, then opens it to reveal four magic flowers that squirt when you squeeze them.

Grandpa gives each of us a beautiful book
about Passover, and we give him the matzoh
so all of us can share it with dessert.

Last of all, Mama opens the door for Elijah, the invisible prophet of hope. Will he drink from the cup we have set for him on the table? The wind gusts, the candles flicker, the wine in his cup wobbles, and when it settles... it seems there is less! Elijah, I wonder, or Uncle Harry?

We sing, holding each other's hands in a large circle of love and then, at last, the seder is over. Uncle Harry kisses Aunt Eda. Uncle Arnold snores in his chair. Sara, Max, and Ben smile drowsily.

And me? I sit wide awake wondering about so many things. About the matzoh ... about Elijah's cup ... about the specialness of the day. What made it all so special? Was it Uncle Harry's magic, or was it ... the magic of Passover?

The story of Passover is a story of freedom. Passover recalls the time, three thousand years ago, when the Jewish people, led by Moses, escaped from slavery. According to the story of Exodus in the Bible, God sent ten deadly plagues down to Egypt before the king, called a pharaoh, finally agreed to let the Jewish slaves leave his land. When the pharaoh broke his word and tried to trap the Jews by the Red Sea, God parted the waters to allow them to cross safely.

Every spring, this miracle of freedom is celebrated with a seder, a festive meal during which symbolic foods are eaten and the story of Passover is retold from special books called Haggadahs. A special seder plate holds bitter herbs — horseradish or lettuce — a reminder of the bitterness of slavery; parsley or other greens, which stand for life and hope; salt water to recall the tears of the Jewish slaves; a roasted lamb bone, which recalls the lamb used in ancient sacrifices; a roasted egg, which stands for sacrifice as well as the promise of new life; and haroses, a sweet mixture of fruit and nuts that resembles the mortar the slaves used when they built buildings for the pharaoh.

When the Jewish people escaped from Egypt, they left in a hurry. They had no time to wait for their bread to rise and so, to honor and remember their ancestors, Jewish people today eat only flat, unleavened matzoh bread during the seder and the following eight days of Passover.

During the seder, to remember that they are free now, everyone may sit or recline on a pillow at the table. In the days of the pharaoh, only people who were free could enjoy such comfort. An extra wine glass, and in some homes, an extra place, is set for the prophet Elijah. Late in the seder, the door is opened in the hope that he will enter and drink some wine. People watch eagerly for him, believing that when he comes, there will no longer be slavery, hunger, poverty, or war.

The story of Passover is a story of freedom — a story without an end. Where Jewish people are free to practice their religious beliefs, they pray that all people everywhere will one day be free.

the FourQuesTions

Why is this night different from all other nights?

- Why on this night do we eat only matzoh?
- Why on this night do we eat bitter herbs?
- Why on this night do we dip parsley into salt water and bitter herbs into *haroses?*
- Why on this night do we recline at the table?